THE MADE DAUGHTER

S.E. Isaac

Monster in the Cookie Jar

Copyright © 2022 S.E. Isaac

All rights reserved.

Cover Designer: Monster in the Cookie Jar

No part of this book may be reproduced in any form or by any electronic or mechanical means including information storage and retrieval systems – except in the case of brief quotations embodied in critical articles or reviews – without permission in writing from S.E. Isaac.

The characters and events portrayed in this book are fictitious or are used fictitiously. Any similarity to real persons, living or dead, is purely coincidental and not intended by the author. This book is sold in print and electronic formats and is licensed for your personal enjoyment only. This book, when in electronic format, may not be re-sold or given away to other people. If you would like to share this book with another person, please purchase an additional copy for each person or use proper retail channels to lend a copy. If you are reading this book in print or electronic format and did not purchase or borrow it through proper channels, then please return it and purchase your own copy. Thank you for respecting the hard work of this author.

**Disclaimer: Translations were completed using Google Translate and as such have not been verified. Poetic license has been exercised in regard to spelling and removal of language-specific characters to facilitate the flow of the story. The use of these translations is to create a mood within the story. However, in many cases, names and dialog are fictional creations of the author and not meant to be translations of other languages.

BLURB

Adrianna Romano's world has been turned upside down. Her father– the head of the Romano Family– and those in his ranks have just been assassinated, leaving her to sit at the head of the table. She's been groomed for this moment; however, with great power comes great challenges. With every decision she makes, eyes are watching. People waiting in the shadows for her to fail so they can take her place. She doesn't know who to trust and fears she will have the same fate as her father.

Savio Rossi has just received word that Mario Romano is dead. The Romano Family has been left vulnerable and Adrianna is now the head of the family. He hasn't seen her in years but that hasn't changed the way he feels about her. She's still the woman who holds his heart and he'll stop at nothing to make sure she's taken care of.

Will Adrianna be able to let her guard down and trust Savio? Or will his attempts make him a target as well?

CHAPTER ONE
Arianna

The sun peeks through the curtains in my office as I go over the numbers in the books. The warmth on my back is refreshing. Things have been hell the past few weeks with my father and his crew slain in the streets of Trenton. A public display of the firepower and strength the Polish Mob holds.

"Franciszek Nowak! You mother fucker!" I scream, slamming my fists down on the desk.

Franciszek Nowak– Polish mob boss– is to blame for everything that happened. He called the shots. Literally. He's the reason my mother had to bury her husband, and my sisters and me our father.

"Are you okay, Boss?" Carlo asks me.

When I took over as the head of the family there was some resistance amongst the ranks. A few didn't want to work for *a girl*. However, they quickly learned that I had more balls than all of them put together and with the squeeze of the trigger, I silenced those who made snide comments or outright refused to follow my orders.

Carlo Russo was my father's soldier. He had shown his loyalty to the Romano Family since I was a little girl. And, when my father was murdered and I took his place, Carlo stood faithfully by my side. It was only right that I promoted him to my right-hand man. He now oversees the ninety-eight soldiers under me.

"I'm fine, Carlo," I sigh heavily. "What's on the agenda today?"

"Not a whole lot. Nothing for you to worry about really. We have it under control, Boss," he said, causing me to lean back in my chair with my eyebrow rose.

"That's not convincing."

"I swear," he chuckles. "Things are pretty quiet around here now that you've taken over."

Quiet? I wasn't sure if that was a compliment or an insult. Did he mean that business wasn't good? Or was he just referring to the fact Popov and his crew hadn't made any more *statements*?

"Boss, it's nothing bad. I swear," Carlo continues, holding his hands up in a surrendering manner. "I just mean that there haven't been any hits or buildings burned in a while. It's a good thing. It means word has gotten around that you're a force to be reckoned with."

"If you tap dance any faster, you might get your cardio in for the day," I smirk, making him laugh.

"Not tap-dancing, Boss. I'm just saying that the city knows that you're…" His words dwindle to nothing. No doubt because he was searching for the right words to use.

"What? That I'm psychotic?" I ask. My head tilted slightly, in a questioning manner.

Benny and Frankie, who are standing guard by the door, nearly die. Their eyes are wide and they choke on the breath they take. They quickly look at Carlo, who also looks mortified.

"Never. I would never call you that. Ever. Boss, I swear. That's not what–" Carlo rambles.

"Relax, boys. I'm only teasing," I laugh. The tension in the room settles. All three of them let out a sigh of relief. "I'm okay with being known as the psychotic one if it means no one fucks with this city."

"They definitely know you don't play, Signorina Romano," Benny smiles.

Everyone under me calls me Signorina Romano or Boss. The two are interchangeable and powerful. They are reminders that I'm no longer my Papa's little girl.

"Good. Because it's really tiresome setting examples throughout the city. Ya know?"

"I told you that I'd do the job, Boss," Carlo states. "You don't need to get your hands dirty."

"I know. I don't mind," I shrug. "I have to earn my keep just like everyone else."

My words earn me grins and nods of respect from the guys. I'd be a liar if I said it wasn't nice to have their respect. Respect isn't a must; however, it makes things easier and safer for me because I know my back is safe turned to them.

The sound of a phone ringing pulls my attention back to the room. Carlo fishes his phone out of his pocket and puts it up to his ear.

"Yeah?" he answers. Whatever the person says has Carlo frowning. His free hand grips the arm of his chair. "What the fuck do you mean?"

My attention is now fully on Carlo and his conversation. Benny and Frankie are pretending to not listen, but they're shitty actors. Definitely not winning any awards for their acting skills.

Carlo continues listening to the person and occasionally responds with short answers. His responses aren't telling me shit. I hate guessing games. He has one more minute before I demand he put the damn call on speakerphone.

"Boss?" Carlo says, pulling the phone away from his ear.

"Yes?" I ask unamused.

"Mikołaj just landed at *J.F.K.*" His words make my blood run cold and my heart pounds like a drum. I take slow breaths to ease the beast inside me, threatening to roar its ugly head. My hands brace the desk and my eyes narrow in on Carlo.

"Please, don't shoot me," he pleads.

"Have him tailed. I want to know every damn detail of that

fucker's day. Every. Fucking. Detail. Understood?"

"You got it, Boss," he nods, then brings the phone back to his ear. "Follow him. Don't let him out of your sight. Send me your location in an hour. I'll send some guys over there for backup. Do not fucking lose him. If you do…" Carlo glances at me then looks out the window. "It'll be in your best fucking interest to not lose him. Capiche?"

Carlo hangs up the phone. I watch his body tense as he slowly brings his attention to me. There's fear in his eyes. Maybe because he thinks my temper is about to get the best of me and everyone in my path will feel my wrath. Or maybe it's just simply the unknown.

"This is good news. We finally have eyes on him, Boss," he smiles. His way of trying to ease the rage he knows is coursing through my veins.

Mikołaj is the man responsible for killing my father. There were many Polish soldiers there that night, but Mikołaj is the one who put a bullet in my father. I know this because he proudly voiced it throughout the city and then high-tailed it out of the country to Poland.

"That fucking pussy," I growl. "I want him brought to me alive."

Carlo stands up and gestures to Benny and Frankie. All three of them stand tall like true soldiers before lowering their heads slightly and saying in unison, "Consideralo fatto, Signorina Romano."

Consider it done.

CHAPTER TWO
Savio

The door closes quietly behind me. I look around the room as I head to the empty chair. There are many people here who I haven't seen in quite some time. They're shocked by my arrival. I can see it in their eyes.

"Ah. Mio figlio è a casa," my father says.

Your son is home, indeed, I think as I continue farther into the room.

"Grazie, Papa. It is good to be home," I bow my head slightly in his direction before taking the seat, my father is gesturing to. The chair is to his right. The spot of the underboss.

"Welcome home, Savio," Renato, one of the caporegimes, nods his head out of respect. The others quickly join in to acknowledge me. Better late than never, I suppose.

"How was your flight?" my father asks, leaning back in his chair. He seems genuinely curious, which is unlike him. The man is merciless and cold-hearted as they come. Maybe he's having a change of heart, now that his days are numbered.

"It was long," I say, turning my chair to face him.

"We will keep this short so you can rest," he assures me with a smile. Those in the room nod their heads absent-mindedly. "We were just discussing the Nowak problem out in Jersey."

Nowak. Franciszek Nowak. The dirtiest, sleeziest mother fucker on the planet. The man is the godfather of the Polish mob and lives by no oath. He showed his true colors when he executed Uberto De Santos and everyone under him, while at a sit-down. A sit-down that was supposed to be friendly. There was no prior beef between the two mobs; however, Franciszek had everything orchestrated down to an art.

Normally, a hit of that magnitude and with such skills would impress me. Not this one. This entire thing has had my stomach in knots for weeks. Mario Romano was one of the many slaughtered that day. A man who I've known since I was a little boy and spent time at his house, playing with his daughters; one who has held my heart since we were children– Adrianna.

I've been stuck tending to business for my father, in Italy, for the past six months. I asked to come back to the states to be there for Adrianna during this difficult time. My father denied my request each time, stating that the Romano Family was no more.

Mother fucker, I curse to myself as I look my father straight in the eyes.

"Shit happens, right?" I reply coolie.

"Exactly," my father grins smugly.

His men have been with me since I left for Italy and have not left my side. They've been like shadows, matching my every step. However, my father is sadly mistaken if he thinks for a second that I'm not trying to make my way to Adrianna. I *will* find my way to her. With or without his blessing.

"We're going to have a sit-down with them," he states, making my blood run cold.

"A sit-down?" It takes everything in me not to reach across the table and shove my fist down his fucking throat. Has he learned nothing about Franciszek and his fucking sit-downs?

"Yeah, it'll be good for business."

He opens the decorative wood box in front of him then pulls out a cigar and places it in his mouth. Renato is quick to snip the end and light it. My father takes a few puffs, causing the end to burn brightly. He lets out a heavy breath and a large cloud of smoke rolls past his lips. The stench of the cigar fills my nose almost instantly.

"Are you not worried that he might try to put a bullet in you?"

I ask. The room fills with laughter to include my father's. I look around at the others and they quickly stifle their laughter. I look at my father.

There you are, you cocky bastard, I think taking in his grin. It's the same grin he has whenever he does something shady and is confronted. He doesn't bother wearing a poker face because he's proud of all of his sins.

"We'll worry about the details later. Just know that I want you there," he says, puffing on the cigar.

"Will you be there?"

"Of course. Franciszek is a good friend of mine," he smirks, confirming what I'm already feeling in my gut. My father has committed the ultimate sin– betrayal.

My father and Mario Romano were like brothers. They grew up together. They were inseparable for as long as I could remember. Our families did everything together. It's why I spent so much time with Adrianna and her sisters. It wasn't until my sophomore year that we moved to a different part of the city and started seeing them less and less.

Il sangue verserà a causa tua, I groan.

Blood will spill because of you.

CHAPTER THREE
Adrianna

"Where the fuck did you get these?" I glare at Carlo and then look back at the picture in my hand. My stomach is in knots and I feel like I'm going to be sick at any moment.

"Trevor's been following a lead for a few days. I didn't want to bring it to your attention, just in case it wasn't true, Boss. I'm very sorry," Carlo replies with his eyes lowered to the floor.

"Don Rossi is in business with Franciszek?" I say through clenched teeth. My eyes are starting to water and all the emotions I have kept at bay for weeks are threatening to spill out. "Leave me!" I scream.

The guys quickly exit the room. Carlo looks back at me as though he wants to say something; however, he bows his head and closes the door behind him, leaving me to my demise.

A scream loud enough to wake the dead leaves my mouth as tears stream down my face. I frantically crumple the pictures then jump to my feet and swipe my hand across my desk. Everything goes flying to the ground.

Knock. Knock. Knock.

"Fuck off!" I yell, kicking my desk with all my might. Excruciating pain radiates from my foot but I don't fucking care. I need pain. Physical pain. Maybe then it'll ease the pain in my heart.

Don Rossi is friends with the man responsible for my father's death. The same Don Rossi who was my father's best friend. He even came to the funeral and helped me lay my father to rest. Now, I'm given pictures taken only hours ago of Don Rossi going into Franciszek's home.

"His fucking home!" I scream. The tears rush down my cheeks. There's no reason to stop them. There's no one around to see them.

They can only hear my rage and later all those who stand in my way will feel my wrath. These pictures have sealed my fate. I am the boss and I will take no fucking prisoners!

***

I've been locked away in my office for nearly an hour since ordering my men out of the room. My nerves have settled. My office is once again clean as though nothing ever happened.

"Carlo," I call out. The door opens almost instantly. Carlo sticks his head into my office. I grin and wave him in. "Just you for now."

"You got it, Boss," he says, closing the door behind him and making his way over to me.

I gesture at the chair across from me. He takes his seat and stares at me with curious, yet cautious eyes. Not that I blame him one bit. If I had just stood outside my boss' door and listened to her go on an hour-long rampage, I'd be on pins-and-needles too.

"Who all knows about these pictures?" I ask, holding them up.

"Just you, Trevor, and myself, Boss," he replies. "I didn't want loose lips."

"Smart move." I lean back in my chair and look at him. "I want twenty-four-hour tabs kept on Rossi."

"You got it, Boss."

"Only Trevor, Benny, Frankie, Malakai, and you are to know about this. Understood?"

"You have my word, Boss," he assures me with a nod.

"Tell the others that the hammer is about to drop. If anyone even looks at me the wrong way, I'll blow their fucking head off."

"I will gladly pass that message on. Been waiting for that, Boss."

"Yeah, I've been far too soft in this game; however, we're going to change that. We're going to make the Romano name something to fear."

"I'll follow you into hell, Boss," he vows, grinning.

"I hope so because we're going to war."

CHAPTER FOUR
Savio

The fucking number has been pulled up on my phone for damn near an entire day. Every time I gather the courage to call, I chicken out. This isn't going to be a simple phone call. This is a call that will change everything. There will be no turning back once that call has been made. I can only hope that at the end of it, she will forgive me.

"You want me to fucking call her?" Paulie asks, reaching for my phone. I quickly pull the phone away from him. He chuckles and throws his hands up in surrender. "Just saying. I'm not scared to call her."

Paulie Camilleri is my cousin by blood and my best friend by choice. He's the one person in this world, who I trust besides Adrianna. There's nothing I keep from him, not even my speculation of my father's role in the death of Mario Romano.

"Adrianna will chew you up and spit you back out," I joke. He shakes his head and laughs.

"That girl has always been cut-throat," he trembles dramatically but quickly turns a serious look towards me. "You honestly think she's going to go easy on you if you tell her what you're thinking about telling her?"

"She's going to hate me, Paulie," I sigh. "And, I can't even fucking blame her."

"Then maybe you shouldn't tell her," he suggests.

"Fuck no. If she finds out that I knew something… anything, and didn't tell her, she'll despise me for eternity. I won't have a chance in hell with her."

"Ha. Like you have any fucking chance now," he teases.

"A better chance than you do," I grin.

"Yeah, yeah live it up. You kissed Adrianna Romano," he rolls his eyes. "Does that shit even count? You guys were like eleven or some shit."

"Oh, it counts. Don't you take that away from me." We both laugh; however, it is cut short when my phone rings. We look down at the screen and our eyes widen.

"You think her ears were burning and she knows we're talking about her?" Paulie asks, frowning.

"No. A thousand bucks says she's already onto my father's bullshit," I groan, hitting accept on the call and bringing the phone up to my ear. "Hey, I was just about to call you."

"Yeah. I'm sure," she growls.

Yeah, she knows.

"You available to meet up so we can talk… privately?" I hold my breath as I anxiously wait for her reply.

"Why were you going to call me, Savio?" she sasses. My name rolls smoothly off her tongue. Fuck, how I've missed hearing her say it.

"I have some information for you," I reply, trying my damndest to keep my cool.

"What kind of information?"

"I'd feel more comfortable if we did this in person. Away from everyone. Just the two of us"

"Yeah cause that sounds like a smart idea," she huffs. "Like I could trust any of you."

Her words echo throughout my mind. Each time they slap me in the face. The woman who I cherish the most, no longer trusts me.

"Adrianna," I say firmly, "you know me better than anyone on this fucking planet. You know I'm a man of my word."

"Yeah. If you had told me that twenty-four hours ago, I would have believed you, Savio. Not now."

"We've known each other since we were little ki–"

"Don't you fucking go there!" she screams into the phone. There's a wave of emotions in her voice. Pain. Hurt. Anger.

"Adrianna," I whisper. "Please. I don't like hearing you like this."

"Don't pretend to know me, Savio."

"I don't need to pretend because I *do* know you. Don't you dare think that my loyalty is anywhere but with you."

"Ha! Your loyalty is with that piece of– It doesn't matter. I'm sorry I called."

"I'm not. I've been wanting to call for quite some time, especially the past few hours. We need to talk, Adrianna. No ands, ifs, or buts. We must talk."

"Did you hit your head while you were in Italy?" she asked, making me smile.

"Did you keep tabs on me?" I grin from ear to ear.

"What? No! He told me you were in Italy," she blurts, but I can tell she's blushing.

"Ah. I see," I chuckle. "Well, regardless, name the time and place. I'll only bring Paulie with me."

"No."

"No?" Paulie's eyebrow raises at my question. "It's Paulie, Adrianna."

"I won't meet with either of you because if you even try to betray me, I'll put a bullet in the middle of your forehead."

"You always were the romantic one," I roll my eyes. "We would never betray you."

"Your loyalty lies in the belly of a snake," she retorts coldly.

"I vowed my loyalty to you when we were kids, Adrianna Amara Romano," I growl at her.

"Ooo. Look at the big man, remembering my fucking middle name. Want a fucking cookie?"

I'm crossed between wanting to laugh at her smart-ass remark and wanting to yell at her for being a fucking brat. How can she question my loyalty? She knows my father and I have never been close. He's raised me to be his prodigy but nothing more. We are blood but not family.

"Adrianna, do you really have such little respect for me?" My voice is soft and my tone calm.

The call falls silent. I check the call and see that she hasn't hung up, she just isn't talking.

"Adrianna?"

"What?" she finally replies.

"What happened to us?"

"You went off and left me behind for better things," she snaps. I open my mouth to argue; however, she isn't done. "Coglione!"

Idiot. She must really be pissed if she's speaking Italian.

"All those years I thought you weren't like the rest. I thought you were– were something better. But I guess this side of the fence wasn't green enough for the fucking Rossi Family. I guess the Romano Family were just peasants to you all this time and you were just pretending to–"

"Enough, Adrianna!" I yell at her. Paulie looks at me as though I have lost my mind; however, he doesn't say anything.

"Who the fuck are you talking to like that!" she screams. "I'll fucking–"

"Paulie and I will be in town tomorrow. Where can we meet

you? It's just the two of us."

"What?" she asks in disbelief.

"Paulie and I are coming to see you. Name the time and place. We'll fucking be there. I'm going to show you that I'm the same fucking person you've known your whole life. I swear on everything."

"Savio," Adrianna sighs.

"Yeah?"

"Ti sei rincoglionito!" *Have you lost your mind,* she screams at me.

"I love it when you speak Italian, Beautiful," I smirk. Paulie rolls his eyes and chuckles.

"You're an asshole," she growls then the call ends. I pull the phone away from my ear and laugh.

"Well, that went better than I thought it would," Paulie grins.

"Yeah. I'd have to agree with you," I laugh. "Let's go grab something to eat and then I'll try calling her back."

"Alright, but it's your death wish."

CHAPTER FIVE
Adrianna

What was I expecting by calling Savio? Maybe I hoped hearing a familiar voice would help piece my life back together. Or perhaps I hoped Savio would wake me from this nightmare. However, talking to him did neither for me. Instead, I was left feeling even emptier.

"How you holding up, Boss?" Carlo asks, leaning against the closed door.

"I'm fine. Perfectly fine." I spin my chair so my back is facing him. Tears aren't filling my eyes, but I know they're coming. "What else do we have on the agenda?"

"There isn't too much on the–"

Someone knocks fiercely on the door, interrupting Carlo's sentence. I turn in my chair and glare. Carlo glares at the door.

"Who is it?" I shout.

"It's Cole, Boss," Cole replies from the other side. I gesture for Carlo to open the door, which he quickly does. Cole walks in. "I apologize for interrupting, Boss."

"What has you banging down my damn door?" I growl.

"Sorry, Boss," he lowers his head slightly out of respect then looks at me. A grin crosses his face, peaking my attention. "We got one of those sons of a bitches, Boss."

"What?" I ask, unable to hide my shock and excitement.

"Kryzs. We got him," he smirks. I jump out of my chair. My hands planted firmly on my desk.

"Where is that mother fucker?"

"He's in the basement. Wrapped up nicely with a bow," he grins, earning a smile from me. I walk around my desk and pat him on the shoulder.

"You did good, Cole," I say. "Lead the way."

A few minutes later, we are standing in the meat locker. It's not a true meat locker. It's just a nickname I gave the basement years ago when I was a little girl. It was the meat locker because it was always freezing cold and people were always being chopped up in it.

My favorite color, I muse.

"I thought you were joking," I chuckle as I look Kryzs over. He is gagged with black cloth and bound to a chair. In the middle of his forehead is a large bright pink bow.

"This was a special present for you, Boss," Cole smiles brightly. The other guys nod their heads in agreement.

"And here it isn't even my birthday," I reply, making them laugh. "Is he dead?"

Kryzs' eyes are closed or swollen shut. His face is beaten up badly and there's dried blood all over him. I can't tell if he's breathing or not because of his thick coat.

"Boss, we'd never bring you a dead present unless you requested it," Cole's eyes widened. He looks as though I've slapped him in the face. "You have my loyalty, Boss."

"I know, Cole. Relax. Geeze. Are we all wound up tight, today?" I groan, rolling my eyes. "So, to answer my question, he's alive."

"Yes, Boss," Toby nods before striking Kryzs in the back of the head.

Kryzs snarls against the gag. His eyes open partially and he stares up at me. An emotion washes over him.

"Do you know who I am?" I ask. He doesn't make a sound, only glares at me. "Take his gag out."

Toby quickly unties the gag from behind and the cloth drops

onto Kryzs' lap.

"Do you know who the fuck I am?" This time my words are coated in venom.

"Suka." *Bitch* in Polish he snarls at me.

With all my might, I slap the shit out of him. He grimaces in pain. His head lowers briefly before he raises his gaze to mine and his eyes narrow in on me.

"No," I shake my head and grin. "Jestem śmiercią." *I AM death.*

Kryzs' eyes intensely search mine for something. Perhaps he's wondering if I'm bluffing or if I'm as crazy as my father was. Has he done his homework on me? Or did he follow Franciszek's order blindly?

When he swallows nervously, I know he's found his answer. The realization has finally sunk in. He knows he's trapped in a cage with a lioness. A lioness who is out for blood.

"Your hands are covered in blood and now it's time to pay your debt," I say, walking over to the counter. My eyes scan the tools laid out across the metal tray. Carefully, I make my selection– pliers.

"Torch, Boss?" Cole asks. I hold out the plier to him and nod. A grin tugs at his lips as he takes them from me. "You're in for a real treat, pal."

"Wait! Don't! I'll give you any information you ask! Please!" Kryzs pleads frantically.

"Please?" I scoff, glaring at him. "Where was this mercy you ask for when you were executing my father!"

"Please. Please, just listen to me. Please." His words are to me, but his fear-filled eyes are locked on Cole. Kryzs sucks in a sharp breath as he watches Cole grab a thick pair of welding gloves and he starts setting up the torch. "Wait! Please! I just follow orders."

"Well, now my men will follow orders."

Kryzs' head whips in my direction. He turns a few shades paler and he shakes his head.

"Please. Please. I can– I can tell you anything. Just ask me. I know it all." His Polish accent becomes thicker with each syllable he utters.

"What information could you possibly have that'll make me spare your life?" I smirk. My guys chuckle and shake their heads in disapproval.

"You have a rat problem."

As much as I hate to admit it, my interest is piqued by his words. I have suspected a rat amongst us even before my father's death; however, it was just a hunch and no proof. It wasn't something I could ask for help investigating because whoever I spoke to could easily be the rat.

"Who says I have a rat problem?" I cock my head to the side slightly.

"You seem like smart girl. You know something is not right." His eyes never leave mine as the words flow from his lips.

This speaks volumes to my soul because there's one thing a person can never hide. That one thing is the emotion in their eyes. No matter how hard they try to mask their feelings, the eyes will never lie.

"Let's pretend for a moment that I'm dumb... enlighten me. What do you know?" I gesture at the empty chair. Carlo grabs it and brings it over to me. "Thank you."

"No worries, Boss," Carlo says, walking back over to the wall and leaning against it. I slowly take my seat.

"Go on. Tell me what it is you think you know."

"It is no think. I know," Kryzs nods his head. "Your rat eats out of many hands."

And the tapdance continues.

In normal conversation, analogies would entertain me; however, my patience is growing thin. Just like everyone else who has been brought down to the meat locker, Kryzs is attempting to buy time.

"Stop talking fucking riddles and tell Boss what the fuck she wants to hear," Carlo growls. The hissing sound of the blow torch being turned on catches all of our attention.

"No. Please. Give me time to tell you," Kryzs begs.

"Better talk fast," Cole chuckles, toying with the height of the flame. Kryzs looks at me.

"Joey!" he blurts. "It is Joey. He is your rat. I swear!"

There are many Joeys on the books, but deep down I know which one he speaks of.

"Which Joey?" I ask, already knowing the answer.

"Joey Roo." He mispronounces the last name the way most people do.

Cole nearly drops the torch he's holding, while the others in the room gasp from shock. I, on the other hand, hold my composure. Or that's how those in the room would see me.

On the inside, it's a different story. The confirmation of Joey being the rat has my emotions crashing against me like a tsunami. Joey Reul was my father's bookie. A man he grew up with since a small boy. My father trusted Joey just like he had trusted Don Rossi.

Sciocco. You idiot, I grumble to myself in Italian, thinking about my father and the mistakes he made.

There was no one in my father's inner circle, who stuck to the honor code. All of them were rats in my book. Well, all but Giovanni Tacchelli, who was my youngest sister's godfather. Rosaline was currently in his care and God help the world if he turned out to be a rat too and something happened to Rosaline. I would burn the world down to ash.

"I see," I reply emotionlessly, not letting my thoughts of Rosaline and Giovanni influence me. I'll deal with all that, if and when the time comes. "And why would I believe you?"

"I have no reason to lie!" Kryzs stares in horror at the flame coming out of the torch that Cole is waving close to the back of his head.

"Ha." I roll my eyes. "You have every fucking reason to lie."

"No. No," he shakes his head. "I bargain."

"Oh. So now you make the calls?" My eyebrow raises and I smirk.

"No. I give you information. You let me go."

The guys look at Kryzs as though he has a dick growing out of his forehead. The man has clearly lost his mind if he thinks he can buy his life that easily. People don't just waltz into the meat locker and leave. Death always follows them. And death *will* come to him. One way or another.

CHAPTER SIX
Savio

When Adrianna had called me back, I had hoped that her emotions were at bay and she had come to her senses. Never in a million years would I have guessed she'd ask me to prove my loyalty to her by bringing her the head of Joey Reul. I had asked if she meant literally or if she just wanted him brought to her. She had replied, *Surprise me*, then hung up on my ass.

"So what are you going to do?" Paulie asks, taking a drag off his cigarette.

"I'd do anything for her. You know that," I shrug. He blows the smoke out the cracked open car window and chuckles.

"Yeah. You've always had it bad for her."

"Fucking understatement of a lifetime," I groan.

"Could just tell her no," he replies. I cut my eyes at him and find him grinning ear-to-ear. "Yeah, I'm just fucking with you. There's no way you'd ever tell her no."

"And you could?" I ask with my eyebrow raised. He rolls his eyes and shakes his head.

"Nope. Adrianna is a force to be reckoned with," he sighs. "I'm not even in love with her like you are and I'd walk through hell for her."

"She's always had our back," I remind him. He nods and takes a slow drag from his cigarette. The cherry brightens as he inhales deeply.

"Yeah. I'll never forget that day," he says, releasing the smoke as he speaks, "you and I got caught stealing the Butcher's car. He was ready to skin us alive."

"Yeah. We were fucking dead meat." My head falls back against the headrest and I picture that day as though it had just happened, and not years ago.

"But little Adrianna caught wind of the Butcher having us. She and Sofia came rushing over with their daddy's guns," Paulie laughs, making me chuckle. "Their scrawny asses demanding the Butcher release us or they were going to blow his fucking head off."

"Yeah, they were fucking nuts," I laugh, glancing at him. He smiles before taking another drag. He releases the smoke-filled breath slowly.

"The Butcher told her, *This doesn't concern little bambinas.*" Paulie's imitation of the Butcher is almost spot on. "Adrianna told him she'd give him until the count of three before she blew his head off."

"He refused all the way until zero," I half-ass laugh as a shiver runs down my spine.

The memory of the Butcher's head being blown off, blood and brains splattering everywhere flashes through my mind. It was the first time I saw death up close. And, Adrianna had been the one who pulled the trigger. She had been only ten years old, just a child, but she risked her life to protect Paulie and me.

"Fuck," Paulie groans. "That whole day was crazy. Her... and Sofia."

Silence falls over us. Thoughts of that day wander across my mind. And I have no doubt it is crossing Paulie's too. That day changed everything and for what? Senseless shenanigans that could have ended our lives and Adrianna and Sofia's too.

"I know Sofia didn't pull the trigger that day," Paulie whispers, "but I have no doubt that she would have. Ya know?"

"Yeah. They both came through for us," I nod. "Our mothers would have buried their sons because the Butcher would have tortured and killed us."

"Yeah, I think about that shit all the time," he grits. "We got fucking lucky."

"Damn lucky." I close my eyes briefly then open them and look at him. "We fucked with the wrong person, stealing his car. We knew better."

Paulie and I knew better than stealing the Butcher's car. Hell, we didn't need his car or the money. Our parents bought us everything we wanted, we went on vacations, and had the world handed to us on a silver platter, yet, we had to have some fun and steal the Butcher's car.

"We were just dumbass kids," he retorts.

"Regardless, Adrianna could have gone to prison or someone from the Butcher's family could have killed her and Sofia."

"I know," he whispers. "That's why they'll always have my loyalty."

"For eternity."

***

"Why do they always fucking cry?" I groan, wiping my hands on a kitchen towel.

"Different breed," Paulie shrugs before lighting a cigarette.

"That shit is going to kill you one day."

"Ha," he rolls his eyes. "Have you seen our life? These cigarettes are the least of my worry. It'll be your pops, who kills me."

If Paulie had made that statement a few days ago, I would have laughed at him. However, things have changed. My father is a much bigger monster than I ever realized. Any man willing to kill his best friend isn't human.

"I won't let that fucking happen. Ever!" I declare.

"Yeah. Like you have the power to stop him," Paulie mutters. "Once he knows where we are, he's going to kill us. You know that."

"I'll kill him first."

Paulie stares at me as though I have a fucking third eyeball in the middle of my forehead. Don't blame him. The words had left my mouth before I even realized it was a thought.

"Do you hear yourself?" Paulie asks in disbelief.

"Just another body," I shrug.

"It's your fucking pops! You can't just kill him!"

"I can if it comes down to him or me."

Loud sobbing pulls my attention away from Paulie. My eyes land on a bound and gagged Joey Reul. He stares at me through swollen eyes with tears streaming down his face.

"You're really fucking pathetic. Ya know that?" I groan. "You fucked with the wrong person and now you have to pay your debt. So stop fucking sniveling."

He whimpers something through the gag but nothing I can fucking understand.

"If he keeps crying, I might just shoot him myself," Paulie pulls out his gun and aims it at Joey.

Joey's body tenses before the waterworks turn on full blast. I open my mouth to yell at him, but a pool of liquid flooding from under him makes me stop in my tracks.

"Did you just fucking piss yourself?" Paulie asks in a half-snarl, half-laugh.

"Jesus. This guy here," I shake my head. "We're gonna need a cleaning crew and we haven't even killed him yet."

It had already taken Paulie and me fifteen minutes to clean up the blood from Joey's busted-up nose. He bled like a stuck pig. Blood was everywhere. It looked like a crime scene.

"Maybe give her a call and see if she has one," Paulie interrupts my thoughts.

"She's the head of the table, now. Of course, she has a fucking cleaning crew," I growl.

Paulie mutters something. I cut my eyes at him and he holds his hands up in surrender.

"Want me to call her?" he asks, putting away his gun.

"No. I'll do it," I fish my phone out of my pocket and let out a heavy sigh. "Let's get this shit over with."

CHAPTER SIX
Adrianna

Knock. Knock. Knock.

My heart skips several beats and I suck in a sharp breath. My entire body fills with nerves at the thought of who is on the other side of the door– Savio.

"What?" I call out towards the steps. The creaks open.

"They're here, Boss," Benny replies down the stairs.

"Bring them down."

Heavy footsteps bound down the steps. With each step, my heartbeat quickens. My stomach knots and nerves fill me.

"Hey," Savio's husky voice cuts through me like a hot knife through butter. If I had been standing, I would have melted to the floor.

"You can come over here. We are wrapping up some things," I reply calmly, gesturing in front of me.

Footsteps approach me and I watch as my guys become uneasy. They look behind me. Attentively keeping their eyes on Savio.

Savio steps around me and to where I can finally see him. A shiver runs down my spine and my thighs squeeze together as I take in the sight of him. All six-foot-three Italian sex god him.

Fuck. Keep it together, Adrianna. It's just Savio, I scold myself internally.

Savio smiles warmly down at me. I fight the urge to rip his clothes off and have my way with him. The Meat Locker is the last place anyone should have sex. It's filled with death… but damn, he looks sexy as fuck.

"Hey, Adrianna," Paulie damn near sings as he comes into view.

"Paulie," I acknowledge. He nods and smiles brightly.

"Haven't seen you in ages. How you holding up? Sorry to hear about your father," he rambles nervously, teetering back and forth on his heels.

I've known Paulie almost my whole life. I know his words are genuine; however, they make my blood run cold. After all, Savio's father is now best pals with the man who had my father executed.

"Paulie," Savio grits. Paulie looks at Savio dumbfoundedly. Savio cuts his eyes at him and the light bulb finally goes off.

"Oh!" Paulie turns to me again. "I am so sorry, Adrianna. I meant no disrespect. I swear."

"You're fine, Paulie," I smirk. "Your mouth always did get you in trouble."

"Uh, that it did," Paulie laughs sheepishly with his eyes lowered to the floor.

"Forget about it," I smile. Savio and Paulie both chuckle.

"Boss, where you want this piece of shit?" Benny asks. I look over my shoulder back at him. He and Trevor are holding up a bound and beaten to a pulp Joey Ruel.

"I see he still has his head," I say, glancing at Savio.

"I'm all for taking it off right here in front of you," Savio replies. Not a single fucking word he spoke should have been sexual to me. Yet, I found myself hornier than ever, wanting him to take it *all* off.

Fuck. I need some damn air, I think, standing up.

"Strip him then toss him in the freezer," I order, gesturing at one of the freezer doors. "Let him sit on ice a bit for his betrayal."

Joey screams against the gag. He flails against the tape binding him. Benny and Trevor keep their hold on him and carry him closer to the freezers. Carlo grabs a knife off the table and then makes his way over to them.

"Want me to give them a hand?" Paulie asks. I don't speak, just motion for him to proceed, if he wishes. He cracks his knuckles playfully then heads over to help.

Paulie glances back at me as he steps over Kryzs' body.

"He isn't dead, yet, if that's what the fucking look is for," I cross my arms in front of my chest. He shakes his head and laughs.

"You're the boss here. I was just wondering if you wanted me to move him or something. He's a pretty big fucking guy and he's taking up a lot of space," he replies.

"No. I'm not done with him. He passed out before I could finish." My eyes lower to Kryzs and I frown. "Fucking pussy."

Savio chuckles beside me, gaining my attention. He steps closer to me. The scent of his cologne wraps around me and I inhale sharply. His amber-colored eyes look down at me. My heart races and suddenly the room feels like it is engulfed in flames.

"Temper. Temper," he whispers close to me. I feel the warmth of his breath against my face.

"Are you trying to get killed by me?" I ask, keeping my composure. He grins.

"Much rather live for you than be killed by you, Adrianna," he replies huskily.

His words were soft but spoke volumes to me. Whether he meant for them to be romantic or not, my heart absorbed them and my mind memorized them. Typical Savio, always turning my world upside down.

"Well aren't you a real Casanova," I roll my eyes, downplaying the warmth and butterfly feeling he's giving me.

Savio Rossi has always been *the one*. When I was little, I told everyone in my family how I was going to marry him. My father told me it was just puppy love. My mother told me how he was no good for me. And my sisters... Well, they'd support me no matter my decision. So any chance Sofia and Rose got, they'd help get me alone with him.

Time went by and a few stolen kisses; however, things never went farther than that. And then his family moved and I saw less and less of him. We still texted and talked on the phone but it wasn't the same as seeing each other. Truth be told, I missed the son of a bitch.

"When we get a chance, I'd like to talk to you alone, Adrianna," he sighs.

"Maybe, once I'm done with business." I turn my attention away from him and look back at the guys dealing with Joey.

Carlo cuts the tape from around Joey's feet, freeing his legs. The moment that happens, Joey begins the fight of his life. Benny and Trevor hold his arms tight while Carlo and Paulie each grab one of his legs.

Joey screams against the gag. His face turns dark red. A vein bulges in his neck and across his forehead. If he keeps this up, he's going to have a heart attack and take all the fun out of the freezer.

"Enough!" I shout, walking over to the group. Everyone looks at me including Joey, who has finally shut the hell up. "Joey, if I hear another sound out of you, I'm going to cut your fucking tongue out. Do you understand?"

His eyes widen and he nods frantically.

"Good." I bend down and look him in the eyes. With a bright smile, I pat him on the cheek, "Now, be a good little rat and let them strip you."

CHAPTER SEVEN
Savio

The door clicks closed behind me. My body tenses as nerves course through me. Years of waiting and the moment has finally arrived. I'm finally alone with Adrianna.

She's in the corner pouring gold liquor from a crystal decanter. She fills two glasses halfway and then places the stopper back in before setting the decanter back on the table. She grabs both glasses and carries them over to where I am sitting.

"Looks like someone could use a drink," Adriana teases, handing me one of the glasses.

"Gratzi," I smile.

"Prego," she says, taking a seat across from me.

She takes a slow sip. Over the brim of the glass, her hazel eyes watch me. No doubt she's contemplating her next move.

"How was Italy?" Adrianna lowers her glass.

"About as well as any forced trip," I groan then take a sip from my glass.

"Yeah, you did abruptly leave the country." Her eyes narrow in on me. Her grip on her glass tightens. Her knuckles turn white. My stomach knots at the accusation that is burning in her eyes.

"Adrianna," I warn. "I didn't know what the hell was going on. One minute I'm sitting poolside at my penthouse and the next moment, I'm being ordered to the airport by my dad."

"I never accused you of anything," she retorts, taking another drink from her glass.

"You didn't need to fucking accuse me. It's written all over your face, Adrianna."

"Stop saying my name as though we're personal," she spats

with a finger pointed at me. "You gave up that right when you walked away from me."

"Walked away? You've got to be fucking kidding me!" I growl and set down my drink. "I never– NEVER– walked away from you!"

"Right. Whatever you say, Savio."

"You know my loyalty lies with you, Adrianna Amara Romano. It always has. Always fucking will." My eyes never leave hers. She needs to not just hear my words but feel them. "Don't question my loyalty, Adrianna."

"Or what? What are you going to do? Spank me?" she sasses.

I place my glass down and without thinking, I reach across and take her glass from her. I place it next to mine then grab her by her arms. With one quick movement, I have her out of her chair and bent over my knees. Her black dress is up over her ass, revealing her red thong and luscious ass.

Smack! The sound of me spanking her fills the room and I find myself bracing for the slap she's about to give me.

"I'm… I'm sorry," I stammer. She looks up at me with red cheeks and lust-filled eyes. My dick instantly turns rock hard.

I had spanked her just to prove a point; however, she's just upped the ante.

"Show me you're loyal to me, Savio," she says seductively.

"Name it and it's yours," I stroke her cheek softly.

"Fuck me," she growls.

"No," I shake my head, earning a death stare from her. "First, I'm going to punish you."

Smack! I spank her hard, leaving a faint red mark on her ass. She arches her back and moans loudly. The most heavenly fucking sound I've ever heard.

Smack!

"Savio!" she whimpers, making my cock ache to be buried deep inside her.

"Does my Italian goddess-like being punished?"

"Please. Punish me," she begs.

Her plea doesn't fall on deaf ears. I slip my fingers through her thong. She lifts up just enough for me to slide them down then she settles on my lap again.

My hand roams across her perfect ass and down between her legs. She parts them wider, giving me access to what I desire most. I suck in a sharp breath when I feel the wetness that is waiting for me.

"Fuck, Baby. You're wet," I moan.

"For you. Only you," she pants.

The smoothness of her pussy teases me as I move my hand slowly up to her clit. My dick jerks inside my pants, threatening to erupt. And, my jaw clenches.

"Fuck," I groan. "So fucking sexy."

"Shut up and fuck me," Adrianna demands, earning her a firm slap to the ass from my free hand. "Savio," she growls.

"You can boss me around when others are looking but not when we are alone. Understand?" I ask, rubbing her ass where my hand had struck.

"Sav–"

Smack. She whimpers softly.

"You don't always have to be in control, Adrianna," I whisper, massaging the redness. "It's okay to relax once in a while and let someone else take care of you."

"Savio, don't," she says in a shaky voice. I look her in the eyes and she turns her head, but not before I see the tears swelling up in her eyes.

How tired and broken she must be. She was thrown to the wolves without a moment's notice. There's no telling what heartaches and pain she had endured by herself.

"Adrianna," I whisper. "Look at me."

When she doesn't face me, I pick her up and cradle her in my arms. She buries her face in my shirt and cries quietly.

"You're never going to be alone again." Gently, I kiss the top of her head. "I promise."

CHAPTER EIGHT
Adrianna

Crying in front of Savio was the last thing I wanted. The tenderness in his voice had broken me. The tears flowed for what felt like an eternity and he didn't complain once. He held me closely, kissed my head, and told me everything was going to be okay. Part of me wanted to run out of the room, while the other part of me wanted to cling to his words with hope and conviction.

When Carlo knocked on the door to check on me, I had ordered him to show Paulie to the guest house and then dismissed the guys for the rest of the day. Carlo was hesitant but followed my instructions, leaving Savio and me alone in the house.

In a perfect world, Savio and I would have had sex everywhere; however, I had cried myself into exhaustion. Savio carried me through the house to my room. He tucked me in and began to leave, but I grabbed his hand and asked him to stay. Strong, independent me had shown weakness. I was completely vulnerable to Savio and I wasn't sure if it'd lead to my demise.

"What's on your mind, Beautiful?" Savio's voice startles me. I thought he was still asleep.

"Just thinking about what I need to get done, tomorrow," I lie thoughtlessly.

"Right," Savio chuckles. "You're a shitty ass liar, Adrianna."

I quickly sit up and turn to face him.

"You think you can just waltz in here and act as though you know me? Do you know how much time has gone by? Do you have any fucking clue what I've been through!" I scream at him. He stares up at me with intense eyes. "Well, do you? Do you have a fucking clue!"

My heart pounds like a drum as my stomach twists in knots.

Savio isn't my enemy. I fucking know that, but I can't help the rage inside me. I'm angry at what my life has become. Angry because despite his father's actions, I still fucking love him.

"Let it all out," he says, pulling me down against him. He wraps his arms around me and kisses the top of my head. "Let it all out, Beautiful. I'm not going anywhere."

I try to fight against him to sit back up. He holds me tightly, shaking his head. If I was to scream, it'd take less than thirty seconds for one of the guys walking the perimeter to get inside the house to me.

"You don't have to hold the weight of the world up, Adrianna. Stop fighting me and let me in," he whispers. His voice is calm. His tone is genuine.

Why can't life be fucking simple? I curse to myself.

"Savio, do you not realize just how heavy this world is?" I groan. "Do you not realize what the fuck I'm about to do?"

"I'm not going to pretend that I know how heavy your world is, Adrianna," he kisses the side of my head and squeezes me tighter. "I don't care how heavy it is be–"

The rage I felt moments ago is nothing compared to what is flowing through my veins now. How dare he lay in my damn bed and talk like this. Who the hell does he think he is?

"What do you fucking mean you don't ca–" He claps a hand over my mouth.

"Ugh. Let me finish, crazy woman." He laughs and lowers his hand. "I don't care because I'm going to help you carry it."

Everything inside me settles. It is soon replaced with embarrassment. Typical hothead me. Always assuming the worst in people's words.

"I'm losing my mind," I sigh, laying my head on his chest. His heartbeat fills my ears. The rhythm is steady and peaceful.

"I'm sorry I couldn't get here sooner," he whispers. "I wanted to be here so fucking bad. As soon as I heard the news. Hell, before then. But my father kept me busy and..." His words trail off. His heart beats ferociously and I can feel his body tense.

"Now you know why," I state, finishing his sentence. He takes a deep breath.

"Yeah. Now I know why." He runs his fingers along my arm. I tremble at the touch. "He didn't call the shot. I don't even think you're on his radar, but... He needs to atone for his sin. Your father was his friend. His *best fucking* friend. How the fuck can he be friends with a man who... Fuck, Adrianna."

He holds me tighter.

"I'm so fucking sorry. So fucking sorry." The tone in his voice breaks my heart. He sounds so defeated. Not typical strong-willed Savio.

"Not your fault," I say, looking up and cupping his face with my hand. He closes his eyes, leans into my hand, and smiles. Slowly, he opens his eyes.

"He's my father," he sighs. "I can't help but feel responsible."

"You aren't responsible for his sins, just like I'm not responsible for my father's sins," I reply, looking him in the eyes. He grabs my hand and brings it to his lips. He presses the softest kiss to the back of it.

"How did I ever let him pull me away from something so precious?"

"Precious?" I laugh, shaking my head. "Have you fucking met me?"

"Adrianna," he groans. "You may have everyone else fooled but I know you. The true you."

"A lot has changed, Savio," I admit in defeat, laying my head back down on his chest. "So fucking much."

"But deep down, you're still the same person. Little Adrianna who fights bad guys like the Butcher," he chuckles. I sit up just enough to look at him. My eyes are wide and my mouth gaped slightly.

"Oh, my God," I giggle. "I forgot all about that schmuck."

Savio's eyebrow raises. He seems shocked or maybe he doesn't believe me.

"Savio, I swear. I forgot all about that guy. Maybe I suppressed the memory or maybe because he was a worthless piece of shit, I purged the memory. I don't know," I shrug.

He sits up and scoots back against the headboard. I'm sure he didn't intend for his dick to be inches away from my face, but it is and my mouth is watering. There's a bulge in his pants, which only adds fuel to the fire.

"Here, sit up so you don't get a kink in your neck," he says, trying to help me up.

"Maybe we should finish what we started yesterday?" I suggest, glancing up at him. He sucks in a sharp breath and grips the sheets.

"You have a lot on your mind. I think you'd feel better if we–" His words cut off when I grab his cock through his pants. I look up at him and grin.

"I think we'd both feel better if we released some built-up pressure."

"Adrianna," he growls. His eyes are filled with a burning desire.

"Savio," I retort wickedly. My finger traces along the outline of his hard-on. "I always wanted to touch you, feel you... taste you."

"Fucking Christ, Adrianna," he moans. "Let's freshen up and then I'm going to show you what happens when you play with fire."

A moan slips past my lips at the thought of Savio finally taking me.

"Move your ass, Savio Rossi," I growl, sitting up and climbing off the bed. I hear him chuckling as I rush across the room toward the bathroom.

"Yes, ma'am."

Minutes later, I'm standing in my room, completely naked, waiting for Savio to finish. The door to the bathroom opens and he steps into the room. His eyes widen as he looks me over.

"Fucking perfect," he smiles, walking across the room, undoing buttons to his shirt with each step. "So fucking perfect."

"I wouldn't say that," I chuckle nervously. He ignores my words and tosses his shirt to the floor. "Fuck."

My eyes wander over his exposed skin. He's covered in tattoos and his nipples are pierced. I lick my lips slowly.

"Like what you see, Beautiful?" Savio asks huskily with a smug grin.

"Love what I see," I step closer to him. "Like what you see?"

He pinches my nipples. A flood gate inside me is opened. My pussy throbs and my knees weaken. I grab hold of his shoulders to keep from falling to the floor. He lifts me and my legs wrap around his waist.

"Wrap your arms around my neck," he orders. I wrap my arms around his neck without hesitation. He works his pants and lowers them to the ground. With me in his arms, he walks over to the bed and climbs onto it. He lowers me gently.

"Take me, Savio," I whisper. He grins and shakes his head. My eyebrow raises. "No?"

"No, ma'am." He lifts my legs and lays on his stomach. My heart skips several beats as his warm breath grazes against my pussy. "I need to eat first."

"Savio," I whimper.

"Relax, Beautiful. I'm going to take good care of you."

"Let me suck you t– FUCK!" I scream, when he lowers his mouth between my thighs. His tongue flicks as his mouth greedily sucks my clit. "Savio."

My hands grip his hair. My hips rock, pressing his face closer against my pussy. So much need and desire are burning in my core.

"Savio. Please. I… Please."

"Let's see how tight this pretty little pussy is," he says huskily then parts my lips with the tips of his fingers. He slides a finger inside me, stretching me. My back arches off the bed and I scream out in pleasure.

"So fucking tight," Savio moans and thrusts a second finger inside me.

"Savio!" I scream, bucking wildly against the bed.

"So. Fucking. Tight," he says, sliding his fingers in and out of me fast and hard. He swirls his tongue around my clit, then sucks it into his mouth without warning.

"Savio! Fuck!" My screams echo throughout the room.

Savio doesn't reply. He just continues torturing me with his tongue, while his fingers fuck me senselessly. With his free hand, he grabs my hip firmly, trying to keep me in place. I look down to find Savio looking up at me.

"Savio. Please. I need your–" My mind clouds with pleasure and lust as he wickedly bites my thigh. "Fuck me! Fuck me now!" I demand, gripping his hair hard. He growls and ignores my words.

My pussy tightens and throbs around his fingers. Countless screams escape my mouth as an orgasm builds. I need this. I need to release. To give everything to Savio.

Just the thought of giving myself to Savio is just the push my body needs.

"Savio! Savio! Savio!" I call out as I erupt. His fingers pick up the pace so does his tongue. He licks, flicks, and sucks my clit greedily. "SAVIO!"

CHAPTER NINE
Savio

Adrianna crying out my name is music to my fucking ears. I've waited a lifetime to please her. To hear my name roll off her lips. To feel her body. To taste her.

I slip my fingers from inside her and replace them with my tongue. The taste of her coats my tongue.

"So sweet," I moan against her pussy.

"Savio," she gasps.

"Yes, Love?"

"Fuck," she giggles softly and looks down at me. Her cheeks are flushed. Her tits raise and lower heavily with each ragged breath she takes.

"You taste divine," I say, placing my fingers in my mouth. She sucks in a sharp breath and watches as I suck her juices off. "Mmm. I hope there will be more of that."

"Fuck yes," she moans. "Now, fuck me."

"So bossy," I chuckle.

"I can find someone else if you don't want to fuck me," she smirks, making me growl. "Jealous?"

"You're fucking mine," I snarl before sitting up on my knees and pulling her closer to me by her legs.

My cock presses against her wet, warm pussy. She moans and grips the sheets.

"Yeah, you better hold on, Beautiful. I'm about to fuck you into oblivion." I grab my dick and position the tip into her wetness.

"Promises. Promises," she tsks.

I don't give her a warning. I thrust inside her pussy. It's so fucking tight that it almost hurts. Adrianna screams out in pain and I still. My eyes lock on hers.

"Adrianna?" I ask softly.

"I'm– I'm fine. Just give me a minute," she breathes heavily. Tears form in her eyes.

Reality sinks in and guilt floods me. I always assumed Adrianna had any man she wanted. Not once did I consider that she was still a virgin. If I had, I would have been gentle with her.

"Am I your fir–"

"Finish that question, and I'm going to shoot you," she snaps.

"Fuck," I groan. "Baby, if I had known, I would have–"

"Shut up, Savio Rossi!" she yells, closing her eyes.

"Baby, I'm sor–"

Her hands reach up and she grabs my throat. She stares up at me with fire in her eyes. Her sudden dominating has my dick even harder. Women bossing me around has never turned me on, but then again, they were never Adrianna.

"Do not fucking apologize. Understand?" she glares up at me.

"Yes, Ma'am," I reply.

"Good." A smirk tugs at her lips and she drops her hands down to her sides. "Now, be a good boy and fuck me."

"Fuck," I moan. "Yes, Ma'am."

I position her legs against my chest and pull out slowly, leaving just the tip inside her. She whimpers in protest. Slowly, I push back inside. Her pussy stretches again, but this time Adrianna moans. She pinches her nipples and stares at me with lust-filled eyes.

"Make me feel good, Savio. Understand?"

Her controlling tone is hard to bear. I want to slide out and then ram balls deep inside her. Next round, I'm going to fuck her hard and fast.

"Yes, Ma'am."

I ease in and out of her slowly until her pussy welcomes me. My pace speeds up and Adrianna rocks her hips to match my thrusts. Her moans of pleasure and my moans fill the room.

"Baby, you feel so fucking good," I say.

"Savio," she moans.

"Pinch your nipples hard," I order. She pinches her nipples and her pussy tightens around my dick. "Fuck yes. Keep pinching."

"Yes, Sir," she whispers.

The vulnerability in her words and her relinquishing control almost makes me bust. One of the sexiest things. Her giving me the power. The power that she lives by.

"Good, Girl," I reply, slapping her ass.

Again, her pussy throbs. She screams and grabs the sheets.

"Hands on your tits, Adrianna," I growl, ramming in and out of her. My hands grip her hips keeping her in place.

"Yes. Yes– Yes, Sir," she moans. Her hands grab her beautiful, big tits.

"Pinch your nipples. Pinch your nipples, right now."

She does as instructed. My balls tighten.

"Fuck, I'm going to come," I groan.

"Come for me, Savio. Fill my pussy," she begs.

"Cum first. Wrap your legs around me."

Her legs wrap around me. I slip my hand between her thighs. The tips of my fingers press again her clit, rubbing small circles against it. Adrianna's eyes close. She arches her back and moans.

"That's it, Baby. Give me what's mine." I thrust in and out of her pussy with need. "Give me what's mine, Adrianna. Now!"

"Savio!"

She shatters around me. Her pussy tightens around my cock and she becomes so wet.

"Come again. Give me more," I growl.

"Fill me. Now!" she demands, looking up at me. "Do as your told."

"Fuck!" I roar.

My body tenses and my orgasm washes through me like a tidal wave. Every drop of my cum releases deep inside her. Not a drop wasted. It's all hers. All of it. All of me.

CHAPTER TEN
Adrianna

I'm seated at the head of the table. To my left is Savio with Paulie next to him. To my right is Carlo. The other chairs at the table are filled with my high-ranking guys.

"There's a sitdown later today," Savio says, looking at me.

"A sit-down?" My eyebrow raises.

"My fath–" He shakes off his words. "Don Rossi is meeting up with Franciszek later, today."

The room fills with uproar. My guys accusing Savio of lying. Paulie defends Savio, while I sit and listen to both sides.

I know Savio isn't lying; however, if he wants to sit anywhere near this table, he needs to hold his own.

"Enough!" Carlo shouts when a few of the guys threaten to kill Savio. "You might not like him, but he's here as a guest to the boss so watch your tone and apologize."

Many would think his order of an apology would be for them to apologize to Savio. They'd be wrong.

"Sorry, Boss," my guys reply in unison. Paulie and Savio look at me. I smirk and shrug slightly.

"What time is the sitdown?" I ask, looking at Savio.

"Five. At Franciszek's," he states coolie. I glance at the clock on the wall.

"We have four hours to come up with a plan."

Savio shakes his head.

"No plan needed." He looks at me. "Just say the word. I'll go to the meeting and take care of it."

"You'd never make it out alive," I remind him.

"That's what Paulie here is for," he glances at Paulie and chuckles.

"I can take care of the guys on the perimeter, while cuzzo here takes care of the inside," Paulie grins.

"You honestly think the two of you can take down... not one," Benny holds up one finger then two, "but two mob families, all by yourselves?"

Most of the room laughs.

"Better than risking any of you," Savio replies, shutting up the entire room. All eyes are on him. "Look, my father is a piece of shit. He didn't make the call or pull the trigger but he might as well have. I'm not going to let anyone else from the Romano Family get hurt. Ain't fucking happening. End of fucking story."

"Well, aren't you chivalrous?" I giggle, making the others laugh to include Paulie and Savio.

"I mean it, Ba–" Savio groans. "I mean it, Adrianna."

"I don't doubt your words." He looks at me and I shake my head. "I question your fucking sanity."

"It needs to be–"

"No. You two won't go there alone."

"Then what do you propose?" He leans back in his chair and crosses his arms in front of him.

"Two different plans. One for your father. And one for Franciszek."

"So you don't want it done at Franciszek's?" Paulie asks. I shake my head.

"No. I'll leave your father to you, Savio. I'll even send a few guys with you for backup." I turn to Carlo. "We are going to that sitdown."

"What!" I'm not sure who yelled it first– Savio, Paulie, Carlo, or one of the other guys. All I know is my ears are ringing from their shouting.

"Enough!" I scream, standing up and slamming my hands against the table. The room falls silent and all eyes are on me. "I will not be fucking questioned. Not now. Not fucking ever. If you don't like how I run things then walk out that fucking door because one more fucking uproar, I'm going to start shooting. Understood?"

"Understood," they reply.

"Boss, you know I support you fully," Carlo sighs. "I just don't want anything bad happening to you."

"Then I guess you better do your job and protect me. Right?" I look at him and grin.

"You got it, Boss," he chuckles. "Looks like we're going to war, boys."

The attitude of the room shifts to a celebration. Bright smiles and cheering. Whether it's forced or not, I don't care. I just need them to play the roles of good soldiers and not question my authority. Franciszek will die and by my hand.

"You sure about this?" Savio whispers, leaning over to me. I sit down and look at him.

"Are you sure you can put a bullet in your own father?" I retort. He rolls his eyes and smirks.

"I'll always choose you, Adrianna."

"I guess we're going to see," I smile sweetly.

"I guess we will."

***

Savio had taken Paulie and twenty of my soldiers with him, but not before kissing me as though there was no tomorrow. It took every ounce of me to keep quiet. I wanted to tell him to forget about killing his father and just stay with me. However, it was something that needed to be done, if there was a future with us. I needed to know his loyalty was with me.

Fuck, Adrianna, I cursed myself.

When had I become so ruthless? Making a man kill his father to prove himself to me. Regardless, if Don Rossi was a piece of shit, who probably knew of my father's death before he did.

"She's not even listening to us," Sofia, my middle sister, laughs.

"Adrianna, what has you so preoccupied?" Rosaline 'Rose', my youngest sister, complains.

"Savio is taking care of things as we speak," I say, lifting my gaze to my laptop screen, where my two sisters are on video chat. They both pale but say nothing. "I was given pictures of Don Rossi with Franciszek. They're good friends."

"Are you fucking serious?" Sofia growls.

"Relax. You're going to upset the baby," I scold her. She rubs her huge belly and sighs.

"I just– I just can't believe Don Rossi would be friends with Franciszek Nowak."

"Sometimes perception is wrong. Maybe, they're not actual friends," Rose replies.

Typical Rose. Always trying to find the good in people. She thinks the world is better than it actually is. Sofia and I are to blame for that. We always protected her from seeing the shitty parts of life. Sheltered her from the horrors it holds.

"Savio confirmed that his father is working with Franciszek," I lean back in my chair. Sofia grins and Rose smiles. "What?"

"Did you finally get laid?" Sofia asks, making Rose giggle.

"She does seem to be in a better mood so I'm going to guess she did," Rose smiles like an idiot.

"Ugh. Are you two really going to do this right now? Do you even care why I called you?"

"No," they both reply, shaking their head.

"Why don't you care about what I have to say?"

"This is much juicier," Sofia gushes and Rose nods. "Besides, whatever it is, we know you have it under control. You always do. You're the boss."

"More like Godmother," Rose corrects her.

"Ooo. I like the sound of that."

"Sound of what?" Antonio, Sofia's husband, asks off camera.

Antonio Berlusconi is the head of the Berlusconi Family. He runs Las Vegas. My sleazy Uncle Tino once tried to run it by using my father's name and Giuseppe De Santis, the mob boss my father worked under. It didn't end well for my uncle.

"Rose said Adrianna is like a Godmother."

Antonio steps behind Sofia and kisses her. He looks into the camera and waves.

"Ladies," he smiles.

"Hey, Antonio," Rose waves.

"Antonio," I acknowledge.

"Godmother does have a nice ring to it, Adrianna. Or should I call you La Madrina?" he grins, making Sofia and Rose giggle like idiots.

"Ugh. Not you too?" I groan.

"It has a nice ring to it," he nods. "The Berlusconi Family supports you fully and would gladly fall under you should you choose to become the Godmother."

"What?" I ask in a hushed voice.

Rosaline looks like she is about to burst with excitement. Sofia is smiling ear-to-ear. Antonio stares into the camera, almost like he's staring into my soul.

"We've been talking about it," Sofia admits. "You have big shoes to fill and need allies, Adrianna."

"And, you'd gladly do that, Antonio? Even though I'm a woman?"

"Geeze, Adrianna," Sofia groans.

"You're family," Antonio laughs. "Besides I take orders from your bratty sister all the time, so what's one more bossy Romano sister?"

I tried not to, but his words actually make me laugh.

"You're so not getting pussy for like a year!" Sofia waves a finger at him.

"Ew. Sofia!" Rose makes a face of disgust, which only makes me laugh harder.

"What? Haven't you gotten laid yet, little Rosaline?" Sofia teases.

"Shut up. I'm going to disconnect the call if you don't stop."

"I needed this," I sigh. They all look at me. Or at least, it feels like their eyes are on me.

"Why don't you let me come back home and you won't be alone?" Rose smiles.

"No," I shake my head. "Not until things are safe here."

"Oh, come on. You're about to take down the bad guy, who killed Papa."

"When things are safe. One-hundred-percent safe, then you can come home. I promise."

"Fine," she looks sad but doesn't argue.

I glance up at the clock.

"I have to go, but I love you both very much," I smile. "Antonio, it was nice seeing you again."

"Like-wise, La Madrina," he grins.

"Really does sound good," Sofia smiles.

"We'll talk more later. I have to go."

"Love you!" Rosaline and Sofia yell, knowing I'm about to disconnect the video call without another word. My finger taps the mouse and the call ends.

Love you too, I think, smiling to myself and standing up. It's time to get the show on the road.

CHAPTER ELEVEN
Savio

The *Towncar* pulls up to the front of my father's mansion. I open the door and my father climbs inside. I close the door and then make my way to the other side of the car. I quickly climb in. Renato, my father's right-hand man, climbs in the passenger seat and we're on our way.

There are two cars in front of us and two following us. They're filled with my father's men. Each one of them swore an oath to lay their life down for them and today they're going to prove it.

"I heard you went and saw Adrianna," my father says, puffing on his cigar.

"I did," I grin.

"Did you have fun?" he laughs. "Another whore."

I punch him in the face without hesitation. He groans in pain and holds his nose. Blood seeps out from his hand.

"You son of a bitch!" he shouts. "Renato! Renato!"

I press the button on the door, lowering the petition between the driver and us. Renato is slumped against the window. My father's eyes grow wide.

"Renato! What'd you do to him?" my father snarls. "Who the fuck are you?

"Apologies. Renato is taking a little nap," Benny, Adrianna's guy, glances back at my father and grins. "A long fucking nap."

Benny turns his attention back to the road.

"You fucking piece of shit! Do you know who the fuck I am?" my father growls, lunging forward to try to grab Benny.

I grab my father by his collar and yank him back down in his seat. He turns on me with murder in his eyes. I pull my gun out of my jacket and point it at him.

"Cut the bullshit! You aren't in charge anymore. We've had a change in… management," I grin.

"And, you think you can run our family? The Rossi Family?" he rolls his eyes. "You're as useless as your mother."

Rage fills me and I strike him in the side of his head with my gun. He shouts in pain. Blood drips slowly from wear I struck him.

"You will not speak ill of my mother, of Adrianna, or about anyone else I care for. If you do, I will not fucking kill you swiftly. I will fucking torture you… slowly."

"Ha. So now you have balls," he sneers. "Been waiting years for you to be my right-hand man. And, now, you decide to grow a pair and team up with that bi–" He cuts his own words short.

"You did the ultimate sin," I remind him. "You betrayed a friend."

"What does Mario being a friend have to do with any of this?"

"Are you fucking kidding me?" My hold on my gun tightens. He has my blood boiling. Even now with him cornered, he still sees nothing wrong.

"Mario was your friend. How could you spend time with the man who gave the order to execute him?"

"It's business," he leans his head against the headrest. "You wouldn't understand."

"Oh, I fucking understand. You chose money over loyalty!"

"Loyalty is a thing of the past. It doesn't put food on the table or keep you out of the morgue."

"How the fuck are you human?" I ask in disgust. "Mario was your *best* friend."

"Business is business," he shrugs.

"That it is, Father," I lift the gun to his head and cock back the hammer. With a silent prayer, I pull the trigger. "That it is."

CHAPTER TWELVE
Adrianna

My phone vibrates as we pull up in front of Franciszek's. I glance down to see a text from Benny. *It is done.* A smile crosses my face. Savio came through. He proved his loyalty and took care of one of my problems. Now, it is time for me to handle the other one.

"You sure about this, Boss?" Carlo asks beside me. I look at him and nod.

"Yes. I have to be the one to pull the trigger," I reply.

"If there is any sign of danger, I'm getting you out of there. You can kill me later Boss," he informs me.

"Yes, Dad," I roll my eyes.

"I'm serious. I would never forgive myself if…" he shakes his head. "If anything happens to you, I won't–" I hold up my hand and he stops.

"None of that. You're stuck with me for a very long time," I grin and he smiles. It's a forced smile, but nonetheless a smile. "How do you feel about being a boss?"

"What?" His eyes widen. "You just said I was stuck with you, Boss."

"You're super uptight today. Geeze," I groan. "We'll discuss it after the meeting."

"Let me have a look around first then you can get out," he says. "They let us through, way too fast, Boss."

"If it'll ease your mind, go ahead," I gesture at his door. He nods, opens the door, and climbs out. The door closes quietly behind him.

A few minutes go by and my door opens. Carlo extends a hand to me. I place mine in his and he helps me out of the car.

"Thank you," I smile.

"No worries, Boss," he replies, closing the door.

"How many?" I ask quietly, looking around nonchalantly. "I've counted nine."

"Eleven. There are two trying to hide in the SUV parked a little ways back, in the driveway," he whispers.

"Easy enough. Did you send off the text?"

"Did it before I opened your door, Boss," he grins.

"That's why you're my right-hand man."

"My honor, Boss."

The front door opens and Franciszek steps out. He's wearing a black suit that barely fits his obese, sloppy body. He slips looks at me and smiles. My stomach knots and my blood runs cold.

Carlo squeezes my hand gently, gaining my attention.

"We need him inside so the others can do the rest, Boss," he reminds me faintly.

"I know. Thanks."

My words probably sound sarcastic; however, I mean them. For a moment, I almost lost my cool and pulled my gun. Carlo is the anchor, keeping my emotions at bay.

"Little Adrianna Romano has come to visit me," Franciszek says in his thick Polish accent. His men laugh, but they're the only ones laughing.

"Oh, look, maiale grasso has come out of the mud to greet us," I retort, making my men laugh. Franciszek and his men look at me clueless. "Sorry. Let me say it in your native tongue. Maiale grasso."

"You dare call our boss a pig!" one of them shouts at me and reaches for his gun. My men draw their weapons and aim at him. Franciszek laughs and gestures for the man to put down his gun.

"You know our language?" Franciszek continues to laugh. "I was impressed with the gift you sent me. I thought someone else translated for you but now I see you speak our language."

The gift he is referring to is Kryzs. Since Kryzs gave me information, I spared his life. Before my guys dropped him off in front of Franciszek's compound, I had *Jesteś następny*- You're next- carved onto his forehead.

"You must have gone to a very good school," Franciszek chuckles. "Chodź do środka." *Come inside.*

"After you," I say, walking up the steps with Carlo beside me and five of my guys behind me. The others will stay outside to execute the rest of the plan. Franciszek's men watch intently as we pass them and enter the house behind Franciszek.

The house smells of golabki- Polish cabbage roll. A smell I could take or leave.

"We were better off outside," Carlo complains softly next to me. I glance at him and smirk.

"Manners," I tease. He rolls his eyes and chuckles.

"In here," Franciszek says, walking into a room. Carlo gestures for me to wait in the hallway. Frankie and him go into the room, along with three of Franciszek's men. I wait patiently in the hallway with the others.

"All clear," Carlo states, poking his head into the hallway.

I step into the room. It's a conference room. Much like mine. There is a long wood table and leather chairs. Franciszek is already sitting at the head of the table.

"Please, have a seat," Franciszek gestures at a chair. I walk around the table and sit in the chair closest to him. His guys step towards me but he laughs and gestures for them to stop. "What harm can she do?"

"Ona jest jego córką," one replies. *She is his daughter.*

"Jest małą dziewczynką.," Franciszek points at me but looks at his men. *She is a little girl.*

My fists ball under the table, but I keep my composure. Being called a little girl only adds fuel to the fire. Franciszek underestimating me will be his biggest mistake yet.

I look back at Carlo.

"Leave us," I state. My guys nod their heads.

"Yes, Boss," they say in unison then leave the room. Franciszek cocks his head to the side. A look of confusion crosses his face.

"This little girl is not afraid of you," I smile.

His head falls back and he laughs like a hyena. He waves his hand towards the door.

"Leave," he orders. His men aren't like mine. They hesitate, sharing looks with each other. "She doesn't even have a portmonetka. She's empty-handed."

"B–" one of them opens their mouth to speak, but Franciszek slams his fists on the table. His nostrils flare as he breathes heavily. Quickly, his men file out of the room. The door closes behind them.

"You have come to kill me?" he asks, grabbing a wooden humidor and opening it. He pulls out a cigar.

"I have," I reply bluntly. He nods his head and then pulls out a cigar cutter.

"And you think it will be simple?" He snips the end of the cigar.

"Very."

He chuckles, placing the cigar in his mouth. I pull a *Zippo* from my dress pocket. His eyebrow raises and he narrows his eyes on me.

"A little girl needs pockets in her dress," I grin, and flip open the *Zippo*.

"I see this." He leans forward for me to light his cigar. The man has no fear of me.

Knock. Knock. Knock.

I close the *Zippo*, never lighting his cigar. He stares at the door then at me. I smile and stand up.

"Come in," I reply.

The door opens, revealing Carlo and the others, who were in the hallway.

"That was faster than expected," I admit with a questioning look. "Outside too?"

"Yes, Boss," Carlo nods.

"We hurried. We didn't like you in here alone, Boss," Frankie replies.

"My heroes," I tease, turning to face Franciszek. "Hope you don't mind. Your list of employees just got shorter."

"What did you do?" Franciszek growls.

My guys step inside the room and away from the doorway. In the hallway, I can see two bodies laying on the floor. Blood is pooled around them.

"Cleanup crew will be here in an hour," Carlo states.

"Good." I walk around the room, looking at the different paintings and objects that fill it. "You really do have some nice things, Franciszek."

"Go to hell," he spats.

"Ha! One day. One day I'll go there and meet up with you," I say, continuing to look over the room. He watches me like a hawk as I make my way slowly around the room over to him once again. "You executed my father in cold blood."

"He was in the way," he glares up at me.

"Well, now he'll be the death of you."

"You don't think the others will come for you?" He leans back in his chair.

"They can try to come for me," I shrug, grabbing the arms of his chair and pushing him away from the table. I lean against the table in front of him. "Right now, you're my problem. And, I'm afraid I won't be able to sleep until you're gone. I'm sure you can understand."

"They will come for revenge if you kill me."

"Well, when that time comes, they will die. But right now, I have come for my revenge."

I extended my hand out to the side. Carlo walks up and places a gun in my hand.

"You really should have searched my men," I shrug and aim the gun at Franciszek. I cock back the hammer. "Would you care to pray to your God before I end it all?"

"You would be so kind?" he laughs.

Bang! The sound of the gun firing echoes in the room.

"Fuck no," I frown, staring at Franciszek. The middle of his forehead has a gaping hole with blood oozing out. His body slumps over and his chair crashes to the floor with him in it.

"You good, Boss?" Carlo asks, walking over to me.

"Yeah. I'm good." My eyes are glued to Franciszek's lifeless body.

For weeks, I imagined this moment. Torches. Hacksaws. Pliers. All these tools had been in my dreams when I tortured Franscizek Nowak. Never did I picture myself ending it so swiftly; however, I had. The nightmare was now over.

"The cleaning crew can take care of the rest," I say, heading towards the door. "Let's go home, boys."

CHAPTER THIRTEEN
Savio

The door opens and I quickly stand. Adrianna walks into the room. She looks worn out but smiles when our eyes meet. I cross the room in a few quick strides as the door closes behind her.

"Adrianna," I say, wrapping my arms around her and kissing her. "I was so worried about you."

"I told you I'd be fine," she giggles. "I thought you were a badass?"

"Fuck no," I shake my head and look down at her. "Not when it comes to you. I'm a big ass softy when it involves the woman I love."

I groan at my sudden confession and Adrianna tenses in my arms. She looks genuinely surprise by my words.

"You thought I was lying all of these years?" I ask, ignoring the nerves that are rising up in me.

"Not lying," she whispers, lowering her eyes. Her cheeks redden. "I just thought you were blowing smoke up my ass."

"Adrianna," I chuckle then lift her chin gently with my hand. She looks up at me and I smile. "I've loved you since we were just kids. I just didn't think I was good enough for you."

"What?" she frowns. "Why the fuck would you think that?"

Her unladylike words make me laugh. Typical Adrianna. Always letting her temper get the best of her.

"You're beautiful, smart, kind… when you aren't killing people," I tease. She rolls her eyes and laughs. "You're perfection in my eyes. I've always seen myself as a nobody."

"Shut up. You're the only man I see," she admits nervously, making my heart skip several beats. "Whatever. You already knew this."

She leans her head on my chest. I rub her back and kiss the top of her head.

"I'd give my last breath for you, Adrianna," I whisper. She leans back and looks up at me.

"You've already proven yourself to me, Savio," she takes a deep breath. "And, I'm sorry… I'm sorry I had you prove it the way I did."

I shake my head.

"No. Don't apologize. My father needed to be stopped. Your father wasn't the first sin, my father committed that didn't sit right with me. It was just the last straw. Then to think of him trying to kill you… Him dying was a no-brainer. I'd do it a thousand times."

"It's not that simple, Savio," Adrianna sighs. "He's still your father."

"No," I shake my head and kiss her softly. "He was a fucking monster. He has been since I was a child. You know that."

She lowers her head briefly then stares up at me again.

"So, what do we do now?" she asks faintly. "I mean… What happens next?"

"Whatever you want to happen." I swipe a strand of her hair behind her ear. "I'm yours for eternity regardless of what you choose to happen next."

"So, even if I didn't want to be with you, you'd– Stop making that face," she giggles.

"I don't like the thought of us not ending up together," I admit frowning.

"Then you should probably…" she prompts grinning ear-to-ear.

"You, Adrianna Amara Romano, are a force to be reckoned

with." She shrugs off my words innocent-like. "Uh-huh. We both know you enjoy getting your way."

"Ask her already!" Paulie shouts from the other side of the door. Adrianna and I look at the door.

"Shut the hell up, already!" I yell back at him. Adrianna giggles and I drop down to one knee. She freezes in place. Her mouth opens but she doesn't say anything. Just stares at me as I fish the ring box out of my pocket and open it, revealing my grandmother's ruby ring.

"Adrianna Amara Romano, we've been through a lot. Some good. Some bad, but nonetheless, together." My voice shakes as I speak from my heart. "There isn't a single day that I want to go by without you by my side. Adrianna, will you make me the happiest man on the planet and give me the honor of calling you my wife?"

"Yes!" she blurts, smiling.

"What?" I ask in disbelief. She throws herself down towards me and wraps her arms around my neck. Her lips crash against mine. I wrap my arm around her waist and indulge in the kiss.

Minutes go by with us lost in each other. When we finally pull apart, we are panting for air.

"I love you, Savio Rossi," Adrianna smiles.

"I love you, future Mrs. Rossi," I say, taking the ring out. She holds out her left hand and I slip the ring onto her finger. "I promise to be a good husband to you."

"And, I promise to be a good wife to you."

"Promises. Promises," I tease, lowering my head and capturing her lips once more.

Adrianna has just made me the luckiest man. I will do everything in my power to protect her. She will never go without and she will always feel my love… until my dying breath.

EPILOGUE
Adrianna

One year later...

Savio sits in the rocking chair, slowly teetering it back and forth. His eyes are glued to the sleeping baby in his arms.

"You're pretty good at that," I say, startling him slightly. He smiles across the room at me.

"How long have you been standing there?" he asks.

"Long enough to see you're good with babies."

"Think so?" he smiles and stares back down at our niece, Carmelia. "I'm scared to death of being a father."

"A little too late for that," Sofia replies from behind me. She rubs my stomach. Savio looks at us.

"Yeah, just a bit," Savio chuckles.

Sofia and I walk into the room. Sofia tenderly takes Carmelia from Savio.

"You are pretty good with babies," Sofia tells him. He shrugs then stands up and walks over to me.

"Not nice to spy." He taps the tip of my nose, making me laugh.

"Wasn't spying," I inform him grinning.

"What do you call it, Mrs. Rossi?" he chuckles and wraps his arms around me.

"Research," I smile brightly.

"Research?" his eyebrow raises.

"Mmhmm. I was researching to see if my husband was going to be a good father like I suspect he will be."

His head dips back and he laughs. When he stops laughing, he looks down at me.

"And what is your conclusion, Beautiful?"

"My conclusion is... *You* are going to be an amazing father," I smile up at him. He blushes slightly. "Just like how you've been an amazing husband."

"You flatter me, Mrs. Rossi," he kisses me softly.

"Maybe I'm just trying to get lucky," I tease, making him laugh.

"Get a room already," Sofia giggles. "Just not this room."

"Well, you heard your sister-in-law, let's go get a room," I wrap my arms around his neck.

"Yes, Ma'am," he replies, lifting me up and cradling me in his arm. He heads towards the door.

"Good man," Sofia laughs. "Follow her every order and you just might survive marriage."

Savio looks back at Sofia and smiles.

"That's the plan. Happy wife, happy life, right?" he chuckles.

"Exactly. You'll be just fine," she informs him with amusement in her voice. Savio turns and carries me into the hallway. "Don't be late for dinner," Sofia calls out.

"We won't!" I shout back. Carmelia cries, making me feel bad for yelling. "Should we go back?"

"No, Ma'am," Savio shakes his head. "Your research is concluded. Sofia is a great mom and will get Carmelia settled in no time. And, in the meantime, we are going to go practice making little Mia a brother or sister."

"You're such a cad," I giggle.

"Cad? Who the hell uses that word anymore?"

"Your wife does," I retort. He kisses me swiftly and laughs.

"That she does." He kisses me swiftly and laughs. "So, should we go practice?"

"Practice makes perfect, Mr. Rossi."

"That it does, Mrs. Rossi."

He carries me to our room and quickly shows me one of the many perks of being his wife.

I never realized the emptiness in my heart could be filled and that I could feel happiness, but that's what Savio did and does. He shows me that life is worth living for. Each day, he reminds me what it's like to be loved whole-heartedly. He was my first love and will be my last.

THE END

SISTER BOOKS

Sofia: Vanished Series: *Vanished in Vegas* by S.E. Isaac

Adrianna: *The Made Daughter* by S.E. Isaac

Rosaline: Flower of the Month Series: *The Hitman's Rose* by S.E. Isaac

Lightning Source UK Ltd.
Milton Keynes UK
UKHW011308050922
408361UK00003B/855